ANASAZI

By Peter Lourie

Amazon
Erie Canal
Everglades
Hudson River
Mississippi River
Rio Grande
Yukon River
On the Trail of Sacagawea
On the Trail of Lewis and Clark
Lost Treasure of the Inca
The Mystery of the Maya
The Lost Treasure of Captain Kidd
Tierra del Fuego

For older readers:
Sweat of the Sun, Tears of the Moon
River of Mountains

THE LOST WORLD OF THE
ANASAZI

EXPLORING THE MYSTERIES OF CHACO CANYON

PETER LOURIE

AUTHOR'S NOTE

The author wishes to thank Chuck Hannaford, archaeologist, Museum of New Mexico, Office of Archaeological Studies, and Dr. Jeffrey S. Dean, University of Arizona, for their close reading of the manuscript. Special thanks to Gwinn Vivian for introducing me to the mysteries of Chaco Canyon.

The term *Anasazi* is a Navajo word meaning "ancestors of the enemy" and refers to the ancient Puebloan people of the Southwest. I use the term in my book because it is familiar. Many archaeologists, however, now use the phrase "Ancestral Puebloan People," which more accurately describes the vanished culture and connects these ancients to their living descendants. The Pueblo people prefer to call their ancestors, in English, simply "the ancient ones."

To learn about other ancient cultures of the Americas, visit peterlourie.com.

To Ann & Nick

Text and photographs © 2003 by Peter Lourie
Additional photographs courtesy of:
Academy of Natural Sciences, Philadelphia: p. 13
American Museum of Natural History: p. 16
Chaco Archive: p. 12 (top)
Museum of New Mexico: pp.11 (left), 20 (right), 26 (bottom), 36 (right), 37 (right)
National Park Service: 29 (left: thanks to Joyce Raab, John Matthews, and Art Ireland)

Published by Boyds Mills Press
A Highlights Company
815 Church Street
Honesdale, Pennsylvania 18431
Printed in China
Visit our Web site at www.boydsmillspress.com

Publisher Cataloging-in-Publication Data   (U.S.)

Lourie, Peter.
        Anasazi : exploring the mysteries of Chaco Canyon / Peter Lourie. —1st ed.
[48] p. : col. photos., maps ;   cm.
Includes bibliographical references and index.
Summary: A photo essay of a journey to Chaco Canyon, New Mexico, examining
Anasazi ruins, culture, and theories of why the Anasazi abandoned the region.
ISBN 1-56397-972-1
1. Pueblos — New Mexico — Chaco Canyon — Juvenile literature. 2. Chaco Canyon (N.M.)
— Antiquities — Juvenile literature.   (1. Pueblos — New Mexico — Chaco Canyon — Juvenile
literature. 2. Chaco Canyon (N.M.) — Antiquities —Juvenile literature.) I. Title.
978.9 /27 21   E99.P9.L68 2003
        2002117181
First edition, 2003
The text is set in 13-point Usherwood Book.

10 9 8 7 6 5 4 3 2 1

CONTENTS

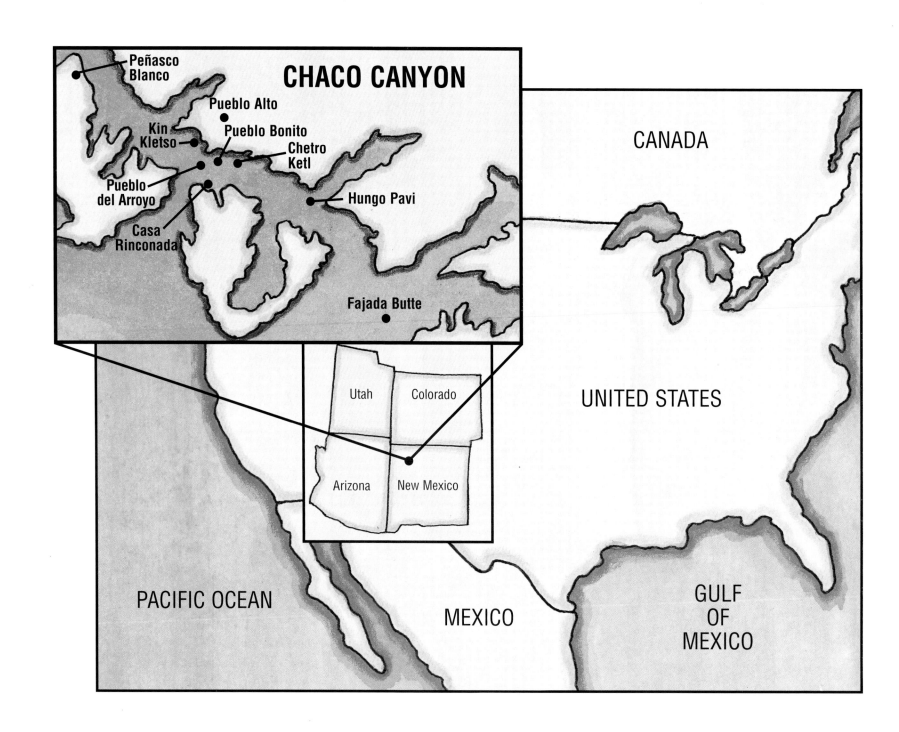

 # PROLOGUE

Around A.D. 1300, in the semiarid Four Corners region of the American Southwest, where Arizona, Utah, Colorado, and New Mexico join, the ancient culture of the Anasazi simply vanished. The Anasazi people, who had flourished in the region for hundreds of years, abandoned their communities and centers of commerce and ceremony.

Why did they leave? Where did they go? Was it an extended drought that made it impossible for them to stay in this rugged land? Did their society crumble from within? The mysteries remain, and scientists are unsure what happened.

Yet plenty of evidence of this once-great culture is scattered about the Southwest. Today the ruins sit empty, roofs collapsed, stone walls crumbling in the desert wind. One thing is for sure: when the Anasazi departed the Four Corners, they left behind a multitude of questions for archaeologists to answer.

Of all the Anasazi sites in the American Southwest, I wanted most to explore the ancient ruins of Chaco. In this remote and barren sandstone canyon in northwestern New Mexico, the Anasazi people built monumental structures that today we call great houses. They were constructed over the period from A.D. 850 to 1150. Most of the great houses were built inside the canyon, but a few stand high along the rim. Thousands of smaller houses and other archaeological sites can be found in the area. Like Mesa Verde with its cliff dwellings farther to the north, Chaco Canyon was one of the most important centers of trade and worship for the Anasazi culture.

Most curious of all, in Chaco archaeologists have discovered a wide-ranging network of roads—about three hundred miles of them. They fan out from the canyon like the spokes of half a wagon wheel, demonstrating how central this canyon hub was to these ancient people.

I asked the archaeologist Gwinn Vivian to guide me through the ruins. Gwinn had grown up in the canyon. His father, Gordon Vivian, first came to excavate at Chaco in 1929. Because Gwinn had been raised here, he knew the area better than most.

With archaeologist Gwinn Vivian.

ONE

A REMOTE CANYON

A sprightly man in his sixties, Gwinn is short and thin, yet he has the energy of a man of thirty. "You will see things this week," he said enthusiastically as he drove me to the canyon on a September day, "that will raise more questions than answers."

The Anasazi who lived in the canyon a thousand years ago, he said, left no written records. All our theories about their culture are devised by looking at stone walls; at leftover timbers; at refuse heaps, called middens; at pots; and at a few burial sites. Much is therefore open to speculation. As a result, Gwinn said, archaeologists don't always agree. Each has his or her own theory about the behavior of the canyon people. "That's the best part about Chaco. It's a land for the imagination."

A VANISHED PEOPLE

At the time of their construction, the massive stone buildings of Chaco, three and four stories high and containing hundreds of rooms, were the largest buildings north of Mexico. Some of them were built over long periods of time, often according to well-established plans, and often oriented to the sun, the

Pueblo del Arroyo: Gwinn and visitors climb the rocks for a spectacular view.

moon, and the four points on a compass. Although these structures were obviously well thought out, no one today is quite sure whether they were lived in or whether they were mostly used as ceremonial buildings.

Archaeologists do agree, however, that after living here for at least three hundred years, the people of the canyon, like all the Anasazi from the Four Corners area, suddenly abandoned Chaco. Scientists believe they probably headed off in three directions: to the east, the south, and the west. The living descendants of the Anasazi are the Hopi and the Zuni people of Arizona and New Mexico, and the Pueblo people along the Rio Grande in New Mexico. One way archaeologists connect these ancient people with the tribes of today is by calling the Anasazi the "Ancestral Puebloan People."

THE CHACO WORLD

On a windswept hill, Gwinn pulled out a satellite image of the San Juan Basin. He pointed to the

The Zuni are descendants of the Ancestral Puebloan People, or Anasazi. Photo taken in 1903.

surrounding mountains, comparing distant landforms to corresponding points on the photograph: "There's Shiprock. There's Mt. Taylor. You see? Mountains on all sides of this basin. And in the center of the basin is Chaco Canyon."

Yes, I could see the sixteen-mile-long canyon in the middle of a huge drainage system called the San Juan Basin in the Colorado Plateau. Most of the water that falls from the skies in this semiarid region passes through the canyon. Although there is often no water

Chaco Wash during the wet season.

11

One archaeological expedition got stuck in the Chaco Wash sometime in the 1920s.

The Chaco world can get frying-pan hot.

here in what is called the Chaco Wash, Gwinn pointed out, that if there was water anywhere in the whole region, it would find its way to this canyon. No wonder the Anasazi chose Chaco for their home.

Gwinn is fascinated with what he calls the "Chaco World." This world did not consist only of the great houses. The Chaco world also included the surrounding environment, the animals, the plants, and of course the climate. Winters are snowy and bleak with temperatures dropping to twenty degrees below zero Fahrenheit. Summers, even today, grow frying-pan hot with long periods without rain. The Chaco world includes badgers, horned toads, whip snakes, bull snakes, prairie rattlesnakes, whiptailed lizards, ravens, wild turkeys, owls, desert cottontails, jackrabbits, coyotes, and large animals like antelope, bear, and deer.

Gwinn thinks the average annual rainfall of today is the same as it was a thousand years ago, only about nine inches. When we drove on the deeply rutted dirt road into the hot desert canyon, I saw big cottonwoods down by the wash but didn't see any water. Gwinn believes the first settlers of the canyon came during a long wet period. They probably established themselves over decades, even centuries. Once they put down roots here, he thinks, even when the climate grew drier and hotter, they stuck it out.

Gwinn explained, "Once settled, the first people who lived in great houses developed early water control systems. I believe their investment was so great that once the climate changed in the 900s, it was difficult for them to leave the area. There was no place nearby that was better. Here they had productive land, and the canyon itself may have assumed a special significance for them."

That sense of place and unity is what continued to keep the Chaco people in the canyon until the mid-1100s when they had no other choice but to leave because of a terrible drought that may have lasted as long as fifty years, which destroyed their way of life.

This is Gwinn's theory—one of many.

FIRST DESCRIPTION
OF CHACO

We set up our tents at the public campground, which sits below the north face of the canyon wall. As darkness spread over the land, the air grew cold. Florence Lister, another Chaco expert, and an old friend of Gwinn's, had come to the canyon where she and her husband had worked for decades. Around the campfire she told how the canyon was discovered by the outside world.

When possession of this area shifted from Mexico to the United States, U.S. troops came to enforce treaties with the Navajo. On one such expedition in 1849, Lieutenant James Simpson, who was a surveyor and mapmaker with an interest in antiquities, became enthralled with the remains of the great houses. For a number of days, he methodically recorded the sites.

Gwinn Vivian by ruin walls.

The ruins of Pueblo Pintado as depicted by Richard Kern in 1849.

13

Ancient walls of Peñasco Blanco stand like sentinels above the canyon.

Two brothers, Richard and Edward Kern, helped Simpson draw and map many of the ruins at Chaco.

Simpson's narrative was the first detailed report on the ruins of Chaco Canyon. Two of his guides helped name the various great houses. Some of these names were Spanish, coupled with strange names like Chetro Ketl. As with so many mysteries of the ruins here, no one has a clear idea where some of these names came from. The word *Chaco* is probably derived from a Spanish corruption of a Navajo word meaning "string of white rocks." Up on the nearby Chacra Mesa, there are some very high buttes that are white.

RICHARD WETHERILL

Chaco's first archaeologist was a rancher from Colorado named Richard Wetherill. He came to Chaco Canyon in 1895 and said that these were the greatest ruins he'd ever seen, and "almost unknown." Wetherill wrote: "I was successful after a few days' search in finding the relics in quantity—the ruins there are enormous—there are 11 of the large Pueblos or houses containing from one hundred to 500 rooms each and numerous small ones. . . . Grass and water is plenty— wood is scarce. A wagon can be driven to the Ruins in 5 or six days from our Ranch."

When Wetherill was able to raise the money, funded in part by the American Museum of Natural History in New York City, he began the first excavations at Chaco. He has been criticized for what many thought was

Richard Wetherill: The first person to excavate Chaco Canyon.

15

Richard Wetherill (right) and colleagues set up camp at Pueblo Bonito. Photo taken between 1897 and 1900.

shoddy archaeological work. But he took good notes and great photographs. He was careful about recording everything he found. From 1897 to 1900 Wetherill excavated Pueblo Bonito, the site with the most number of rooms and the best-excavated Chaco great house. He found thousands of pieces of pottery, stone tools, and turquoise. A number of people thought he was simply looting and that his procedures weren't very scientific. In 1900 his excavation was closed down. Wetherill then went into ranching.

His life came to a sad end in 1910. While he and a cowboy were driving cattle through the canyon, a local Navajo man ambushed them. Bad blood had flowed between the cowboy and the Navajo. The Navajo fired at the cowboy, but the bullet hit Wetherill instead.

One cold, clear morning, I visited the grave of

A lonely place.

Richard Wetherill's grave.

Richard Wetherill. It is situated just under the cliff wall near Pueblo Bonito, the great house where Richard began his first excavation more than a hundred years ago. His gravesite seemed a lonely and forgotten place, surrounded by its little fence. But Richard Wetherill's name is embedded in the history of Southwest archaeology. Not only was Wetherill the first to excavate here at Chaco, he and his brothers were the first to make the now-famous cliff dwellings of Mesa Verde important to the community at large. The Navajo even gave Richard the nickname of "Anasazi" because of his fascination with the ancient culture.

 # TWO

GREAT HOUSES

Between 1921 and 1927 at Pueblo Bonito, one of the most beautiful great houses at Chaco, Neil Judd, working for the Smithsonian Institution, removed 100,000 tons of rubble and windblown sand. He also restored broken walls. Today this great house is perhaps the best known of them all. As I approached the ruins, I found signs asking visitors to enter with respect. For the Hopi and other present-day descendants of the Anasazi people, Pueblo Bonito is a sacred site, a place in which to pray to their ancestors.

Pueblo Bonito, Spanish for "Beautiful Town," was built in a D-shaped manner. Some archaeologists say that the lines of the walls connect to the arcs of the sun and moon as they rise and fall through the sky, especially on those all-important solstices and equinoxes.

Built between A.D. 850 and 1150, Pueblo Bonito once stood five stories tall, and contained more than 650 rooms, forty-five smaller kivas, and at least two great kivas. Kiva is a Hopi word for a special room or structure used for religious and social ceremonies in today's pueblos. Archaeologists use the word *kiva* for prehistoric structures, usually round and dug into the

Pueblo Bonito.

A view from inside an enclosed kiva.

An artist's depiction of the great house known as Hungo Pavi as it may have looked centuries ago.

ground, often with benches, roof support columns, and ventilators. These prehistoric structures were probably used for ceremonies and domestic activities like sleeping, cooking, and eating. Although kivas are exposed today, they would have been covered with timber and mud roofs in the days when the Anasazi lived here.

From the cliff above, in the early morning light, Pueblo Bonito seemed like some futuristic spaceship in the desert. There is a central wall in the great house along a north-south axis that divides the interior of Pueblo Bonito into two plazas. Built with the canyon wall at its back, blocks of multistoried rooms sit on the north, east, and west flank of these two main plazas.

Anasazi masons were expert craftsmen.

In modern-day Pueblo society, kivas and plazas are important places for ceremony and trade, for gathering and daily activity. Within the two plazas at Pueblo Bonito, the great kivas look like two large perfectly round craters. Great kivas are found in almost every Chaco great house built between A.D. 900 and 1200. The central locations of these kivas lead archaeologists to the conclusion that they were very important places for people to assemble and to worship. They are large enough for hundreds of people to enter at the same time.

I followed Gwinn through the main plaza of the great house. We climbed through one room after another and looked up at wood beams that had been here for a thousand years.

As we walked through the ruins, I noticed the fine masonry of the walls. Up close, the walls are indeed beautiful. They show a distinctive quality of Chacoan architecture called "core-and-veneer." The core of the walls is made of roughly shaped pieces of sandstone with mud mortar. Then both sides of the core are faced with more finely shaped pieces of stone, forming the veneer. Different styles of veneer indicate different periods of construction.

These walls in ancient times, however, would have been plastered smooth on the outside. The fine work on the interior, which is now exposed, was not perfected in order to bring attention to the craftsman himself, but it was done in honor of the creator.

The great kiva at Chetro Ketl.

Chetro Ketl.

CHETRO KETL

Not far from Pueblo Bonito, we came to Chetro Ketl. Of the thirteen great houses at Chaco, Chetro Ketl is the one that covers the most acreage. Around A.D. 1010, it probably started out with only one square structure, but by the 1100s it had grown into a site that takes up three acres. Again the structure was designed in the form of a giant D with the front wall of the plaza forming the arc of the D. This great house was constructed with as many as fifty million pieces of cut

The great kiva at Casa Rinconada.

and shaped sandstone. There may have been five hundred rooms in the three-story structure. Like most of the great houses, it contained many smaller kivas and two giant kivas sitting in the wide plaza.

Archaeologists surmise that up to 225 timbers were used for one great kiva. These would have been spruce, fir, Douglas fir, aspen, and ponderosa pine, which grow high in the surrounding mountains. Cutting and transporting these big trees wasn't easy. The logs had to come from at least sixty miles away. Only small juniper and piñon grew around the canyon itself.

CEREMONY AT CHACO

I walked up to the great kiva at Chetro Ketl and looked down into the ceremonial chamber, now roofless. I thought about those who gathered here deep in the earth, covered from sight. I pictured them sitting in ceremony with a juniper wood fire blazing at the center of the chamber.

For the Anasazi, ceremony and spiritual life were a part of day-to-day living, just as they are today for the modern Pueblo people. Archaeologists cannot "see" ceremonies in the ruins. They can merely analyze the objects they find and imagine how those ceremonies looked.

Gwinn showed me a special place around the backside of the great house, where his dad had been excavating when suddenly he discovered a room with loads of ceremonial objects, like painted wood and nonfunctional arrows. He called Gwinn's mom in Albuquerque and asked her to take Gwinn and his two sisters out of school immediately, to get them here to help excavate. "We liked getting out of school," Gwinn told me.

NIGHT IN THE CANYON

Sleeping in my tent in this canyon under a full moon was a gift in itself. Coyotes whined and yipped. The sky was ablaze with a million stars when the moon had found its way over the southern ridge. It grew so large as it rose that it looked as if it would burst. At this general time of the equinox, a special time of year for both the Anasazi and modern Pueblo people, I noticed that the sun and the moon followed nearly identical tracks, rising in the southeast and setting in the southwest, one following the other like a faithful dog follows its master. Hardly had the moon gone down behind the cliff, when, a few hours later, the sun lifted its regal head above the canyon. The desert sun took away the chill of the near-freezing night.

ANNUAL CYCLE OF LIFE

The Anasazi carefully observed the paths of the sun and the moon, and most likely they built their houses and kivas in relation to celestial phenomena. The sun, moon, and stars marked important times of the year, for planting, harvest, and ceremony. Harmony with the

Camping in the canyon.

Moonrise in Chaco Canyon.

This photo of a Zuni pueblo was taken in 1903.

earth and heavens insured good crops and survival. For present-day Pueblos, maintaining harmony with the cycles of the year is important. Archaeologists thus infer that it was similarly important to the people of Chaco Canyon.

PETROGLYPHS AND PICTOGRAPHS

Early the next day, we took a long, hot walk on the canyon floor to a distant site. Peñasco Blanco is an unexcavated great house that stands high above the northwestern end of the canyon.

We walked for hours in the sun, following an old wagon road. I drank frequently from my water bottle, but Gwinn was like a camel. I never saw him drink once.

Petroglyphs and pictographs lined the north canyon wall. After much study and speculation, scientists are not certain what was meant by the ancient artwork. The earlier rock art from 1500 B.C.–A.D. 200, Gwinn called Archaic. These are pictographs, stick figures painted on the rock, often in dark red ochre. The Puebloan period from A.D. 500 to 1150 is characterized by petroglyphs, which are figures etched into the rock. Puebloan art makes up the bulk of Chacoan rock art. Many of these images are of mountain sheep.

The more recent rock art, Gwinn pointed out, dates from the arrival of the Navajo. Stylistically distinct, these drawings are often pictorial narratives, hunting

Petroglyphs.

Scientists are uncertain what such ancient artwork means.

SUPERNOVA AND PEÑASCO BLANCO

scenes, stick figures, horses, and geometrical shapes.

Walking along this gallery of art connected me to the past. I pictured native artists at work, alone and silent as they brought the rock to life. In the slanted orange light of New Mexico, the rocks took on a wonderful vibrancy at that altitude of seven thousand feet above sea level.

We walked past the yellow flowers of the chamisa plant. Salt cedar and coyote willow lined the Chaco Wash along with old Fremont cottonwoods.

A mile or so later we came to a large rock overhang, a place to get out of the drill of the sun. Gwinn pointed to the most spectacular pictograph of all. On the ceiling of the overhanging rock, (and undiscovered until the 1970s!) were three images right next to each

In 1054 an unusually bright star appeared in the sky. An Anasazi artist recorded the event in this remarkable pictograph.

other, painted in distinct red—a crescent moon, a hand print, and a star bursting. Painted probably by the people of Peñasco Blanco, the pictograph is believed to be an Anasazi rendition of the supernova of 1054. The hand print may have been the signature of the artist.

We climbed out of the canyon up to a wonderfully windswept site of mostly unexcavated buildings. Peñasco Blanco felt very different from the other great houses. Gwinn said that only ten percent of the ruins of Chaco had been excavated. It was a strange feeling to walk through an unexcavated site like Peñasco

A view from above the outlier Kin Bineola.

Blanco, and to know that under my feet, under this or that mound of earth and stone rubble, lie Chacoan treasures that may never see the light.

On our return from Peñasco Blanco, the sunset turned the gallery of rock art to the color of blood.

Gwinn points to evidence of a prehistoric road.

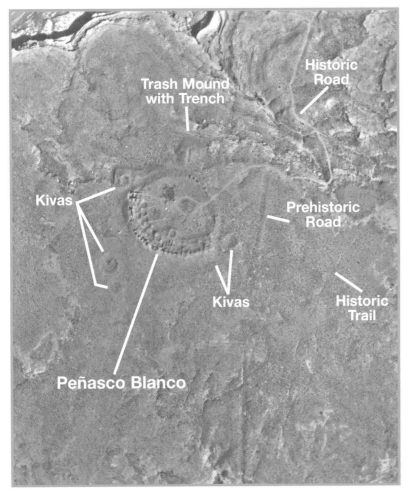

An aerial photo shows kivas, trash mounds, and a prehistoric road.

ANCIENT ROADS

At our campsite that night, Gwinn talked about his discovery of the road system at Chaco. At first, Gwinn and his father had mistakenly thought some of the roads were actually irrigation canals. But in 1970 while walking over the "canal" that leads out of the canyon and up to Pueblo Alto, Gwinn came across steps carved in the rock. That's when he knew he had found a road, and not a canal.

After that, patterns and evidence of roads and also of real canals became clear to Gwinn. In certain contexts, aerial photographs showed canals; and in

A staircase carved out of stone.

smaller great houses outside the canyon that Gwinn planned to show me tomorrow.

The coyotes began yipping at midnight and I couldn't sleep. I had plenty of wide-awake time to think about what I'd seen so far. I kept coming back to a new idea. As a child, I had wanted to dig among the ancient ruins of Inca and Maya civilizations. I had wanted to find stuff—masks, gold, treasures. I had assumed that finding was the greatest work of archaeology. But Gwinn was helping me understand that beyond the digging and finding, there is much work to be done, like analyzing data, or posing and attempting to answer hundreds of questions. Archaeologists are sleuths. They are detectives with limited physical evidence to use as a basis for their elaborate theories. And their theories are merely suggestions of what might have happened.

THEORIES

Gwinn explained in more detail how theories about Chacoan roads reflect differences in theories about how the Anasazi people lived in the canyon. In the 1970s and 1980s, when the road systems were first analyzed, they were thought to be paths for trade and ritual. Other theories about the roads soon developed.

Roads might have been built for moving and storing food. Or they might have been used to bring goods into the great houses for ceremonies. A military theory sees the roads as ways to move troops and supplies from

other contexts they marked ancient roads. Gwinn was careful to caution me, however: "It's still a confusing business to know with any certainty."

Now that we were only a few days from the equinox, that special time of year with equal hours of night and day, I imagined thousands of supplicants approaching the canyon on these roads from the outliers, the one place to another. Part of this theory comes from the fact that the width of the roads, which is often thirty feet, is the same width as Roman roads, which were used for similar troop movement. The cosmic theory holds that the only purpose for the roads was to mark the ground for celestial observations.

Gwinn, who likes to draw from various theories, believes in the idea of the roads as unifiers. One could call this the unity theory. In times of drought and difficulty, the roads may have been ways to get food to the great houses in the canyon from the outlying areas and communities. Gwinn does not think the great houses were used for ceremonial purposes alone, but that actual populations lived there. Other archaeologists disagree.

THE BREAKUP
OF CHACO CANYON

When the population grew and times got tough, Gwinn theorizes, the Anasazi living in the canyon could not produce enough food. So they traveled outside the canyon and built what archaeologists call outliers, which were simply small great houses. Gwinn thinks these outliers were established first for farming. But by the 1100s, because of drought or overpopulation, Gwinn thinks the situation in the canyon was so bad that the Anasazi decided to move people farther out, sending whole segments of the population from great houses like Pueblo Bonito and Chetro Ketl to already

established outlier sites. This would have been a two- or three-day walk.

This theory of Gwinn's maintains that the system of life at Chaco, inside the canyon, operated well for three hundred years, but then it began to break apart. So roads were built as a reminder of the culture's unity. The roads from the outliers, he pointed out, lead back to specific great houses in the canyon, perhaps to the very ones that the people there were originally from. Gwinn thinks the roads acted as reminders that the center of the Chaco universe was still the canyon itself.

In explaining all these theories, Gwinn seemed excited by the guesswork. After all these decades in the canyon, he said with a grin, "It is easy to come up with ideas, but very hard to evaluate those ideas—given such limited evidence."

Stone walls here at New Alto are all that remain of a once-thriving society.

THREE

OUTLIERS AND SMALL HOUSES

The road leading out of the canyon was rutted. It had been nearly destroyed by August rains. We opened and closed the gates of fences used to keep the Navajos' cattle from wandering. Mesas and buttes punctuated the wide-open range. We came across occasional corrals, but saw no one. Although the Navajo have occupied this region for four hundred years, the land is sparsely settled.

The outlier called Kin Klizhin, or "Dark House" (Kin in Navajo means "house" and Klizhin means "dark"), is a small unexcavated great house. Although only two stories high, it is built with the same architectural design as the great houses in the canyon itself.

Around 1080, Kin Klizhin was one of the small great house outliers in a fertile zone, producing food for itself. Perhaps some of this food was carried on the roads to Chaco Canyon. One road from Kin Klizhin heads northeast back to the canyon, but another goes south to an outlier called Kin Bineola.

WHERE THE WIND WHIRLS

As we drove through Navajo land, we passed some Anasazi ruins that had been converted by the Navajo into a Navajo hogan or living house. At Kin Bineola, an outlier with a Navajo name meaning "House Where the

Stone and timber: the fine work of Anasazi craftsmen.

The kiva at Kin Bineola.

An arrowhead unearthed from the desert sand.

Pottery shards: evidence of the Anaszi.

Wind Whirls," Gwinn pointed out an elaborate water control system. We followed the canal away from the buildings. Gwinn said, "Some insist this is a 'ceremonial pathway,' but I am sure it is water control." And the reason he knows this, he said, is from aerial photos. "The signs are subtle, but if you keep checking the aerials you begin to see a pattern." This, I realized, is exactly what archaeologists do—they look for patterns. If you live out here enough years, you see patterns. From those patterns theories are born. As we walked away from the main site into the vastness of greasewood, Gwinn pointed to evidence of part of the canal where his dad had dug years ago. We came across some curious slabs of stone lined up on end, remnants, Gwinn said, of where the Anasazi had channeled water.

POTS AND REFUSE HEAPS

I picked up broken pieces of thousand-year-old pots. With reverence, I held these fragments of black-on-white pottery, geometrical designs. Gwinn said that when I picked up potsherds I had to replace them exactly where I found them. I wondered why I couldn't take a little piece back to my children. Gwinn said that if everyone took just one piece, then Chaco would be robbed of the clues that might help future archaeologists understand what happened here. Also, American Indians believe that the artifacts of the ancients belong where they are. At Chaco, as at all national park sites, the artifacts, plants, animals, and rocks are protected

The Anasazi crafted beautiful pots. Potsherds are strewn throughout many sites in the canyon.

These pots, made by descendants of the Anasazi, give us a good idea of what Anasazi pottery may have looked like. Photo taken in 1925.

by law. So I was careful to place these potsherds in the exact place I'd found them.

I discovered the largest number and variety of potsherds in refuse heaps. These are not like our modern garbage dumps. The Anasazi believed all their earthly belongings had spiritual life and that once a pot, for instance, was broken, it should be placed here in this refuse heap, so that it would be safely preserved for future worlds, the afterlife. The Anasazi buried their dead in these refuse heaps, too.

Gwinn suggested I come back someday to help with a survey. Archaeologists sometimes conduct ground surveys of the surrounding land. They walk for hours, for whole days, ten feet apart from one another, recording everything they see. Miles and miles of walking in the hot sun, ten hours a day. But archaeologists love to be outside and many of them love these surveys. I decided I would like to come back to help survey this vast land. So much was waiting to be discovered.

A potter carries on the tradition of his ancestors in this photo taken in 1940.

FOUR

CHACRA MESA AND FAJADA BUTTE

On our last full day at Chaco, we drove to a special spot high above the canyon where tourists rarely go. Chacra Mesa lies to the southeast. Years ago, whenever they had some spare time, Gwinn and his father came here together to survey the mesa. Those explorations paid off. On Chacra Mesa they found outlier sites never before recorded.

We got out of the van at a site called Pueblo Pintado, or "Painted Pueblo." Gwinn pointed to a wall that had toppled over. Then we knew we were in the refuse heap because all around us were pot handles and beads and shards from different time periods. We even found a jasper projectile point, perfectly formed, thick stone, red and orange in the bright sun.

For lunch we drove a long way to an unnamed canyon at the back of Chaco. We drove over barbed-wire fences, past seemingly uninhabited Navajo ranches. This was cowboy country. The wild smell of sage filled the air. That Gwinn knew his way out here testified to his lifetime knowledge of the rugged back-country. Along the canyon rim there were piñon and juniper trees.

A magnificent sight: Fajada Butte.

At the far south end of the Chacra Mesa, we walked out to the cliff. I strolled off to take some photos. I noticed the distant mountains that surround the San Juan Basin. And at the edge of the cliff I suddenly thought I saw a big brown bear staring at me.

I stopped in fear. I backed up. I was about to run, when I realized it wasn't a bear at all, but rather a gargantuan Ponderosa pine stump. It looked a lot like a bear charging. Behind the "bear" I spotted a conical rock as big as a car. Something told me the bear was a sign that there was some spirit here and that I was meant to stay away.

Later I was told that on top of that conical rock there was a hollowed-out area, perhaps made by the Anasazi. Overlooking the wild unnamed canyon at the back of Chacra Mesa, I thought to myself that maybe this place had been a sacred spot for Anasazi ceremonies long ago.

COUGAR SIGHTING

As we were leaving Chacra Mesa, driving through some rough country, a large cat bounded across the road. Gwinn hit the brakes. I jumped out with my cameras and ran after it into the brush, but it had disappeared. I'm sure it was a young mountain lion. It had a long bushy tail with a black tip and spots.

In the van again coming off the mesa, Gwinn said: "We'll never know exactly what happened in Chaco. And for one, I hope never to solve all these mysteries. Because it is the mystery of the place that brings people back here to ask questions . . . always to ask more questions."

A MYSTERY

Chaco is indeed a great mystery. And nothing creates a better sense of wonder at the Chaco phenomenon than a morning walk on the cliff top above the canyon. Below, I could trace the giant Ds of

The mystery of the Anasazi continues to bring people back to the canyon.

Anasazi masons at Pueblo Bonito worked for the glory of a higher spirit. They never intended their interior work to be seen.

Gwinn points to the Great North Road that drops into Kutz Canyon. This road runs all the way from Chaco Canyon some forty miles south.

the great houses. What incredible buildings! The vision of Pueblo Bonito from above with its many kivas like pockmarks on the moon convinced me again of the sacredness of the place. No wonder the Anasazi stayed as long as they did, through droughts and famine.

Here, too, was Fajada Butte in the distance, that lone and lovely tower of stone that sits in the middle of the canyon. The butte is like a magic icon, visible for miles around, stark and immensely attractive. Now

Pueblo Bonito.

considered a sacred site, only native people are allowed to climb up Fajada Butte to what may well have been a prehistoric celestial observation tower.

In the 1970s, an archaeologist named Anna Sofaer made a startling observation about three slabs of stone at the top of the butte. On certain days and certain nights, the light from the sun and moon, she discovered, passes exactly through the slabs to touch a spiral petroglyph carved there. Apparently, this happens on the all-important solstices and equinoxes. Sofaer believes the celestial observatory on Fajada Butte was the actual center of the universe for the Chaco people. Gwinn told me he himself was not sure he believed in all of the celestial theories made by other archaeologists, but he was willing to accept some of them.

As I walked back to camp along the canyon floor, I thought how Gwinn had been a perfect guide for an introduction to the Chaco world. Although he might have spent more time at Chaco than most archaeologists, Gwinn never seemed to hold his elder statesmanship over the newcomers. For decades, his opinions and theories had evolved as new evidence came to light.

As I took one last look across the dry landscape heating up with the rising sun, I felt an overwhelming awe for the place and the people who had lived here, and for all the scientists who kept coming back to this dry, rugged land in order to solve one of the great mysteries of all time.

Kin Kletso, or "Yellow House," looking south across Chaco Canyon.

FURTHER READING

The books I recommend are mostly for young readers, but I have included a few books intended for older readers as well. These books, filled with photographs, may be of interest to those who wish to find out more about the Anasazi. When I was a kid growing up in Canada, I remember thinking there was a dividing line separating adult books from those for children. I yearned to cross the line. Having crossed over somewhere between fourth and eighth grade, I realized that there was no clear division. Robert and Florence Lister's book, for instance, is a classic for adults as well as children. Of similar interest is Florence Lister's book written in collaboration with Lynn Wilson. The books on the Navajo, Pueblo, and Zuni purport to be for younger readers, yet they would inspire most adults to better know the native people of the Southwest. Another resource is *Mystery of Chaco Canyon*, a film produced by Anna Sofaer, presented by South Carolina ETV, Columbia, South Carolina (1999), and available on video. The Anasazi people should not be thought of as some isolated culture of a vague and distant past. In fact, the Ancestral Puebloan People of a thousand years ago are very much with us today, living in their descendants, in the living traditions of the people who make their home along the Rio Grande and in the Four Corners region of the Southwest.

Arnold, Caroline. *The Ancient Cliff Dwellers of Mesa Verde*. Houghton Mifflin, 2000.

Dutton, Bertha, and Caroline Olin. *Myths and Legends of the Indians of the Southwest: Book II: Hopi, Acoma, Tewa, Zuni*. Bellerophon Books, 1998.

Goodman, Susan E., and Michael J. Doolittle (photographer). *Stones, Bones, and Petroglyphs: Digging into Southwest Archaeology*. Atheneum, 1998.

Griffin, Lana, Tommy J. Nockideneh, Herman J. Viola, and Felix Lowe. *The Navajo (Indian Nations)*. Raintree/Steck Vaughn Publishers, 2000.

Ladd, Edmund J. *The Zuni (Indian Nations)*. Raintree/Steck Vaughn Publishers, 2000.

Lister, Robert H., and Florence C. Lister. *Those Who Came Before—Southwestern Archaeology in the National Park System*. Southwest Parks and Monuments Association, 2000.

Lister, Florence C., and Lynn Wilson. *Windows of the Past: Ruins of the Colorado Plateau*. Sierra Press, 1993.

Strutin, Michele, and George H. H. Huey. *Chaco: A Cultural Legacy*. Southwest Parks and Monuments Association, 2000.

Vivian, R. Gwinn, and Margaret Andersen. *Chaco Canyon (Digging for the Past)*. Oxford University Press, 2002.

Yue, Charlotte, and David Yue. *The Pueblo*. Houghton Mifflin, 1990.

INDEX